This book is dedicated to pretend birthday celebrators everywhere!
HAPPY BIRTHDAY TO YOU!
—L.K. (and C.M.H.)

First Edition • 10 9 8 7 6 5 4 3 2 1 • F850-6835-5-10258
Printed in Singapore • ISBN 978-1-4231-3776-4
Library of Congress Cataloging-in-Publication Data on file. • Reinforced binding
Visit www.hyperionbooksforchildren.com
and for birthday crafts, visit www.lanakittiesbestbirthday.com

THE BEST BIRTHDAY EVER!

YOU ARE INVITED

(ALL PRETEND BIRTHDAY CELEBRATORS EVERYWHERE!)

TO HAVE A PARTY!

HAPPY BIRTHDAY TO YOU!

LOVE,
LANA

(AND C.M.H.)

By ME (Lana Kittie)

(and Charise Mericle Harper)

Disney • HYPERION BOOKS
New York

A birthday only happens one time
in a whole entire year.

On your birthday, you should be
princess of the world!

You should not be
sad and lonely,

sitting in a
time-out
because of →
bad birthday
manners

on the steps, all alone.

That is why it's good to practice party manners with lots of pretend birthdays first.*

1 THE BIRTHDAY INVITATION

Send an invitation to everyone you want to have at your party.

Use lots of fun colors. →

PARTY
TODAY
FOR ME

*Plus, it's fun.

Even if you want to be nice, you should probably not invite everyone in the whole world.

BEES

I love a good party.

Me, too!

pointy stingers

BEARS

Oh, no!

will eat all the cake.

BUSINESSCATS

Good idea!

Let's have a meeting.

Let's all talk numbers while we eat cake.

very boring

On your birthday, no one should be the boss of your fashion except you!

Purrfect!

3 WELCOMING A GUEST

This is a good way to welcome a party guest.

Please come in.
This is going to be
a **great** party.

I'll just put this
in the gift pile,
and then we can
go and play.

This is not a good way to welcome a party guest.

Yay!
Another present FOR ME!

Don't bother me.
I'm resting with my presents!

BIRTHDAY FUN

A good party hostess does not ask her guests to. . . .

. . . and that is why I am so beautiful.

. . . listen to her sing two hundred lovely songs she made up all by herself.

I call this my Rainbow Day Outfit. My Rainbow Night Outfit is next.

. . . watch her do an Amazing Fashion Show.

This is my special rock which I found outside by the fence right after it had rained and . . .

. . . look at her special Important-to-me collection.

Because even though these are excellent things,
listening and watching and looking are not as fun as doing.

Yay! Everybody dance!

A good birthday hostess
chooses something everyone
can do together.

After fun, everyone will be hungry for . . .

5 BIRTHDAY FOOD

A good birthday hostess does not serve . . .

The most important food of the whole day is . . .

6 | **THE BIRTHDAY CAKE**

Candles show how old you are.

Real candles have real fire, pretend candles do not.

The most important song of the whole day is . . .

7 | **THE BIRTHDAY SONG**

8 BLOWING OUT THE CANDLES

No one should ever help you blow out the candles unless you really, really  want them to.

Guests who might blow out the candles by accident should stay away from the cake.

9 OPENING PRESENTS

It takes lots of practice to open a present.

Mostly it's hard because it's important to make the present giver feel happy about the present they gave you.

Wow! Underpants!

I love underpants. Thank you! I wear them every day!

↑ happy present giver

This is what can happen if you don't practice:

I hope it's something good.

I see something.

unhappy present giver

A good party hostess says good-bye to all her guests.

Bye.
Thanks for coming.

Don't forget
your goody bag!

little treats for guests to take home

A good guest does not
try to sneak off with
one of the presents.

HOW TO MAKE A BIRTHDAY CROWN

A birthday crown is kind of like a birthday hat, only better, because it is more fancy and special.

What you will need: Paper ☐, tape or a stapler ◎ ▭, Crayons or markers ▐▎▌, and lots of imagination ☺ !

STEP 1. Make a long, thin strip of paper. ▭ You might have to tape two or more pieces of paper together.

STEP 2. Put the paper strip around your head to get the right size.  Tape or staple the paper together in a ring so that it fits your head without falling down around your neck.

STEP 3. Decide what kind of decoration your crown will have. Cut the decoration out and tape it to the paper ring. Here are some crown ideas:

Birthday Cake Crown

Jeweled Crown

Rainbow City Crown

Flower-Top Crown

Superstar Crown

Happy Balloon Crown